Don't Let the Pigeon Drive the Bus!

Hi! I'm the bus driver. Listen, I've got to leave for a little while, so can you watch things for me until I get back? Thanks. Oh, and remember:

Don't Let the Pigeon Drive the Bus!

words and pictures by mo willems

SCHOLASTIC INC.

New York Toronto London Auckland Sydney
Mexico City New Delhi Hong Kong Buenos Aires

ISBN 0-439-70180-5

Text and Illustrations copyright © 2003 by Mo Willems. All rights reserved. Published by Scholastic Inc., 557 Broadway, New York, NY 10012, by arrangement with Hyperion Books for Children, an imprint of Disney Children's Book Group, LLC. SCHOLASTIC and associated logos are trademarks and/or registered trademarks of Scholastic Inc.

12 11 10 9 8 7 6 5 4 3 2 1   4 5 6 7 8 9/0

Printed in the U.S.A.   40

First Scholastic printing, September 2004

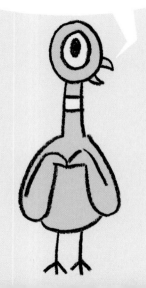

LET ME THE